Tiara Saurus REX

Brianna Caplan Sayres • illustrated by Mike Boldt

BLOOMSBURY
NEW YORK   LONDON   NEW DELHI   SYDNEY

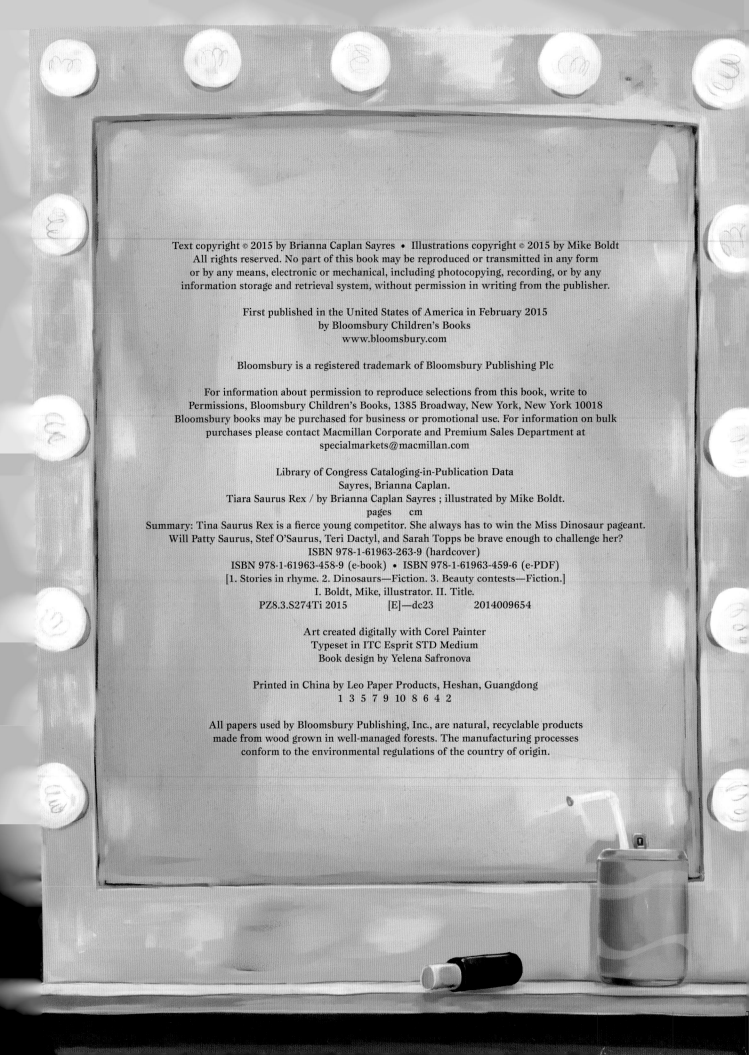

First published in the United States of America in February 2015
by Bloomsbury Children's Books
www.bloomsbury.com

Bloomsbury is a registered trademark of Bloomsbury Publishing Plc

For information about permission to reproduce selections from this book, write to
Permissions, Bloomsbury Children's Books, 1385 Broadway, New York, New York 10018
Bloomsbury books may be purchased for business or promotional use. For information on bulk
purchases please contact Macmillan Corporate and Premium Sales Department at
specialmarkets@macmillan.com

Library of Congress Cataloging-in-Publication Data
Sayres, Brianna Caplan.
Tiara Saurus Rex / by Brianna Caplan Sayres ; illustrated by Mike Boldt.
pages   cm
Summary: Tina Saurus Rex is a fierce young competitor. She always has to win the Miss Dinosaur pageant.
Will Patty Saurus, Stef O'Saurus, Teri Dactyl, and Sarah Topps be brave enough to challenge her?
ISBN 978-1-61963-263-9 (hardcover)
ISBN 978-1-61963-458-9 (e-book) • ISBN 978-1-61963-459-6 (e-PDF)
[1. Stories in rhyme. 2. Dinosaurs—Fiction. 3. Beauty contests—Fiction.]
I. Boldt, Mike, illustrator. II. Title.
PZ8.3.S274Ti 2015   [E]—dc23   2014009654

Art created digitally with Corel Painter
Typeset in ITC Esprit STD Medium
Book design by Yelena Safronova

Printed in China by Leo Paper Products, Heshan, Guangdong
1 3 5 7 9 10 8 6 4 2

All papers used by Bloomsbury Publishing, Inc., are natural, recyclable products
made from wood grown in well-managed forests. The manufacturing processes
conform to the environmental regulations of the country of origin.

For Matthew Saurus
—B. C. S.

For my beautiful Naomi Saurus,

who always wins my heart.
—M. B.

Dino pageant day is here!
They stampede through the door.
Each creature hopes that she'll be crowned
the next Miss Dinosaur.

They put their lipstick on with care,
give their mirrors one last stare.

But makeup artists warn, "Beware . . .
Tina has to win."

Patty Saurus dresses up
to show off all her splendor.
In velvet gown and four-inch heels,
she seems a strong contender.

Stef O'Saurus wows the judges
with her back of shining jewels,
since emeralds on each giant plate
are well within the rules.

Could Tina's lovely big brown eyes
make her the one to beat?
Her brilliant smile seems to say,
"Don't bother to compete."

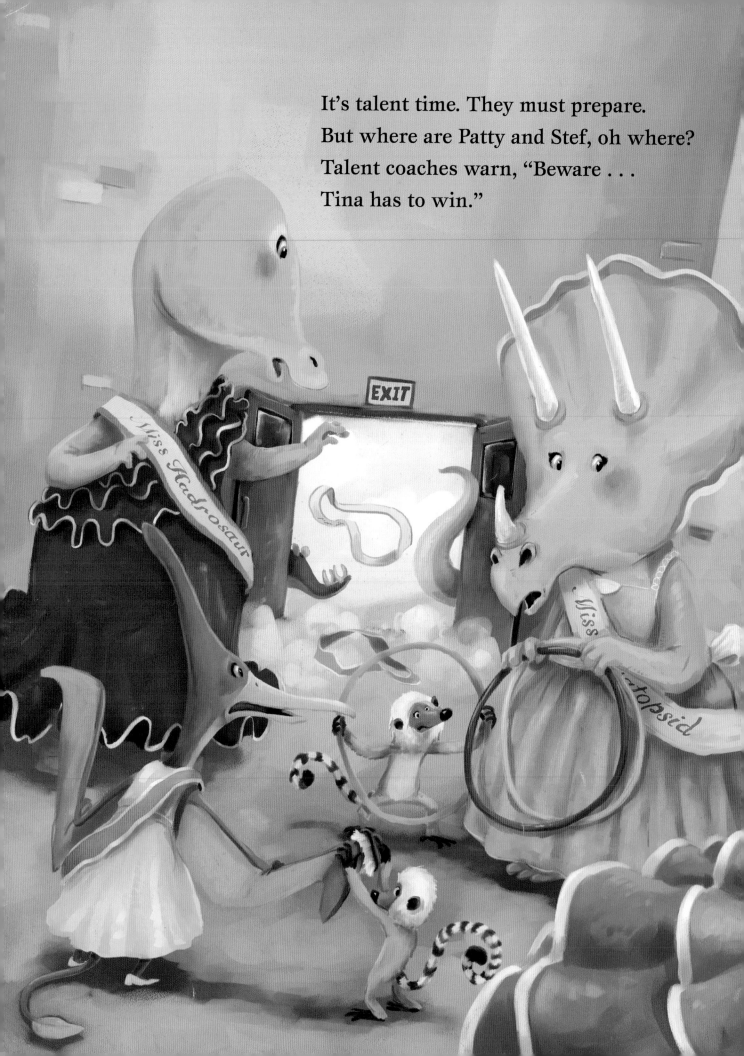

It's talent time. They must prepare.
But where are Patty and Stef, oh where?
Talent coaches warn, "Beware . . .
Tina has to win."

Teri Dactyl spreads her wings
and glides around the room.
The judges burst out clapping
as they watch her graceful *zoom*.

One Hula-Hoop is tough for some,
but Sarah Topps whirls three.
This trick's a breeze for Sarah—
they're on her horns, you see.

Tina holds her partner tight
and tangos round the floor.

She gives a graceful curtsy
as he scurries out the door.

Backstage, wide-eyed girls compare:
"Weren't Sarah and Teri over there?"
And trembling stagehands warn, "Beware . . .
Tina has to win."

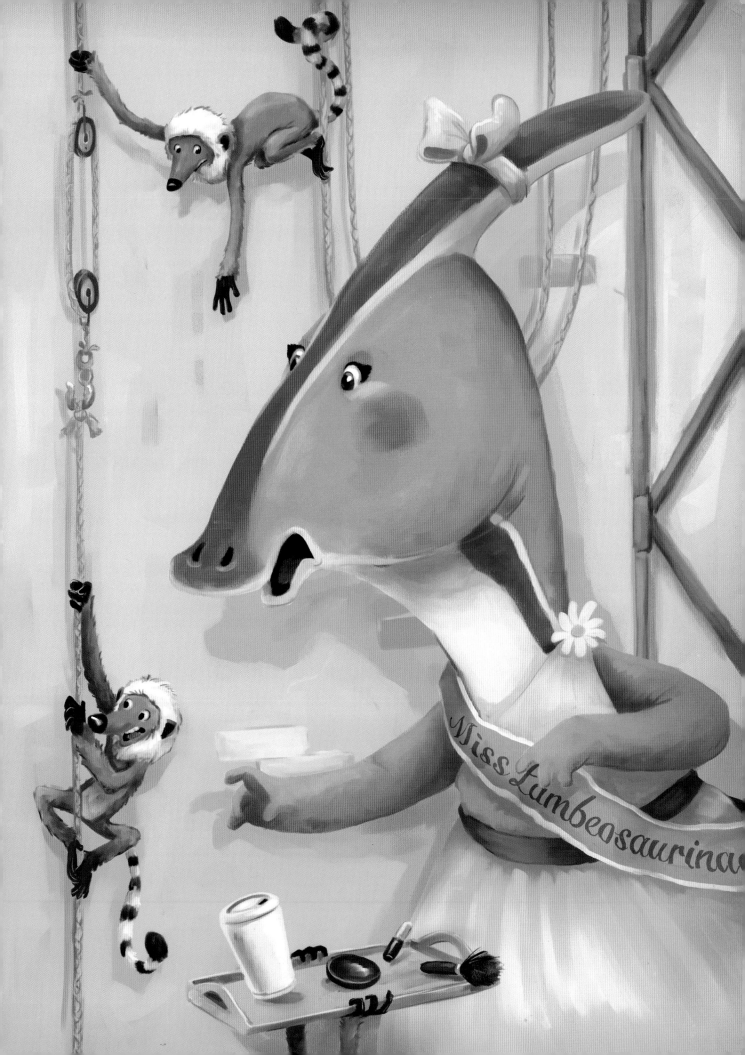

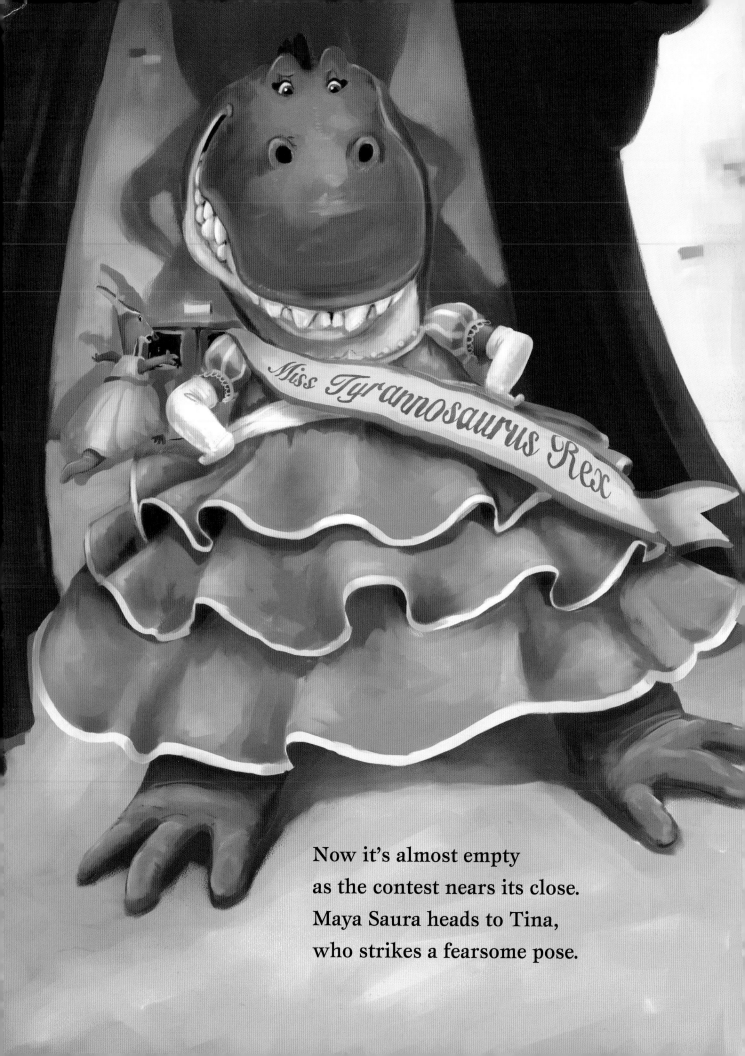

Now it's almost empty
as the contest nears its close.
Maya Saura heads to Tina,
who strikes a fearsome pose.

"What a tango!" exclaims Maya.
"Dino-wow! You sure can dance!"
Tina cracks a tiny grin.
Should she give this girl a chance?

The crowd listens to the drumroll
as the curtain starts to rise.
Who, oh who, will be the one
to win the dino prize?

A judge climbs up a ladder,
adds a crown to Tina's pearls:
"This crown could be for only you . . .
There are no other girls."

But Tina spots one gentle dino
who did not run away.
"Maya Saura!" exclaims Tina.
"Would you like a crown today?"

Then she gives her crown to Maya
for the day's surprising end,
and the lovely Tina Saurus Rex
dino-hugs her new best friend.

They're quite an unexpected pair—
two dino beauties with rare flair.
She shares her crown,
but still beware . . .

Tina always wins!